The Long Wait

Story ✧ Budge Wilson
Art ✧ Eugenie Fernandes

Stoddart Kids

This book is for
Mr. Wilson
Glynis Marie
Andrea Kathryn
and
the Schuttenbelds
— B.W.

Text copyright © 1997 by Budge Wilson
Illustrations copyright © 1997 by Eugenie Fernandes

Stoddart Publishing gratefully acknowledges the support
of the Canada Council and the Ontario Arts Council
in the development of writing and publishing in Canada.

Published in Canada in 1997 by Stoddart Kids,
a division of Stoddart Publishing Co. Limited
34 Lesmill Road
Toronto, Canada M3B 2T6
Tel (416) 445-3333 Fax (416) 445-5967
e-mail Customer.Service@ccmailgw.genpub.com

Published in the United States in 1997 by Stoddart Kids
85 River Rock Drive, Suite 202
Buffalo, New York 14207
Toll free 1-800-805-1083
e-mail gdsinc@genpub.com

Canadian Cataloguing in Publication Data

Wilson, Budge
The long wait

ISBN 0-7737-3021-4

1. Cats – Juvenile fiction.   2I. Fernandes, Eugenie, 1943–   II. Title.
PS8595.I5813L66 1997   jC813'.54   C96-930450-1
PZ7.W55Lo 1997

Printed and bound in Hong Kong

For Mary Lou
— E. F.

    This is a true story about something that really happened. It is a story about Deirdre.

    Deirdre was a black cat. If you want to know how to say her name, try saying DEAR-DREE. Deirdre lived with Mr. and Mrs. Wilson, Marie, and Kathryn. The Wilsons often called her "Dear Deirdre" or "Deirdre Dear". Deirdre was ten years old. Ten years is a pretty long time for a cat.

People who didn't know her, said that Deirdre was not a special cat.

She did not have a sleek and velvet coat.

She did not have a lean and graceful body.

She did not walk like a queen with her head in the air.

But to the Wilsons, Deirdre was special in other ways. She had a big tummy, and when they held her, she felt warm and comforting in their arms. There were no sharp claws or bones sticking into them. Deirdre had a round, serious face. Her left ear had a split down the middle, and her nose looked as though it were made of black leather. She had a purr so loud, it was almost a rattle.

Deirdre loved the Wilsons. Sometimes it is said — mostly by dog lovers — that cats do not care about people. Deirdre cared.

She followed Mrs. Wilson everywhere, even when she went out for walks. Sometimes she cried and meowed until someone patted her. Deirdre often seemed to need love more than she needed food.

When any of the Wilsons came home, Deirdre was always waiting on the braided mat in the front hall. Or, if she was outside, she would flop down on the sidewalk and ask to have her tummy rubbed.

Deirdre loved it when one of them was sick, because she could snuggle up to the sick person all day long.

Deirdre cared about her family a whole lot.

Every summer, Deirdre traveled from Ontario to Nova
Scotia and back again with the Wilsons. Sometimes she went by
plane. Other times she rode by car in a big cat cage. Deirdre
hated the car and she hated that cage. Whenever she was put
inside it, she would tremble all over, like a small, black earth-
quake. Then she would howl for almost the whole trip. Deirdre
was a very well traveled cat.

Then one year, a terrible thing happened.

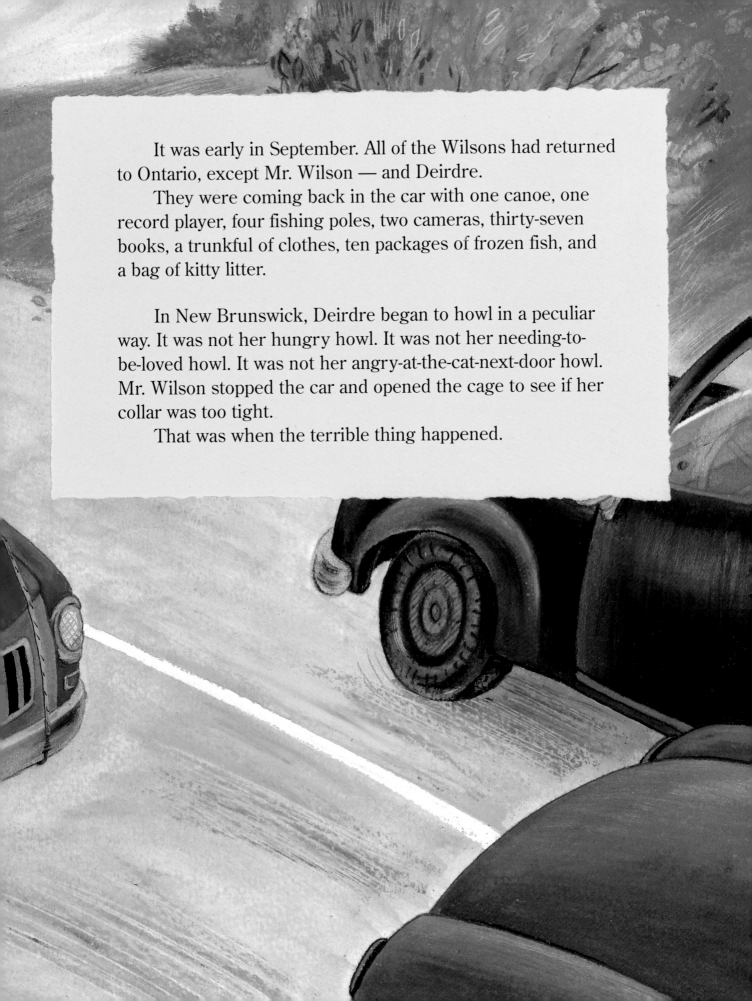

It was early in September. All of the Wilsons had returned to Ontario, except Mr. Wilson — and Deirdre.

They were coming back in the car with one canoe, one record player, four fishing poles, two cameras, thirty-seven books, a trunkful of clothes, ten packages of frozen fish, and a bag of kitty litter.

In New Brunswick, Deirdre began to howl in a peculiar way. It was not her hungry howl. It was not her needing-to-be-loved howl. It was not her angry-at-the-cat-next-door howl. Mr. Wilson stopped the car and opened the cage to see if her collar was too tight.

That was when the terrible thing happened.

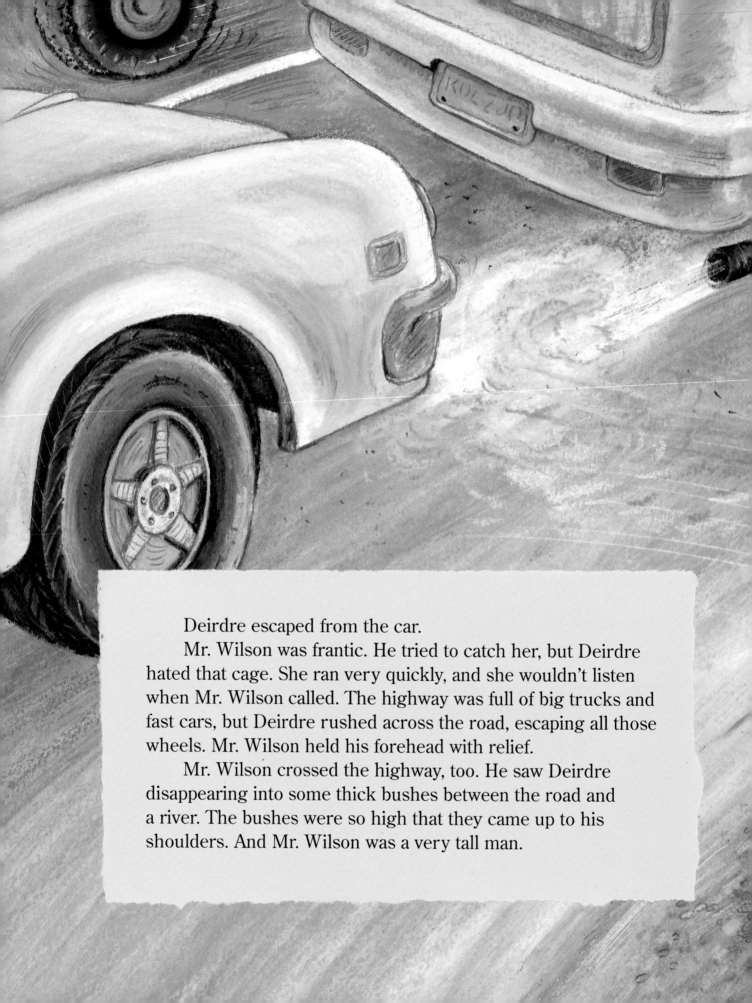

Deirdre escaped from the car.

Mr. Wilson was frantic. He tried to catch her, but Deirdre hated that cage. She ran very quickly, and she wouldn't listen when Mr. Wilson called. The highway was full of big trucks and fast cars, but Deirdre rushed across the road, escaping all those wheels. Mr. Wilson held his forehead with relief.

Mr. Wilson crossed the highway, too. He saw Deirdre disappearing into some thick bushes between the road and a river. The bushes were so high that they came up to his shoulders. And Mr. Wilson was a very tall man.

Mr. Wilson pushed through the bushes and scratched his hands on the branches, trying to find Deirdre. Once he saw her and leapt through the air in a flying tackle. He landed on a rock. His dark glasses fell off and broke. His best grey trousers were covered with stains. When he got up, he had a sore chest — but no Deirdre.

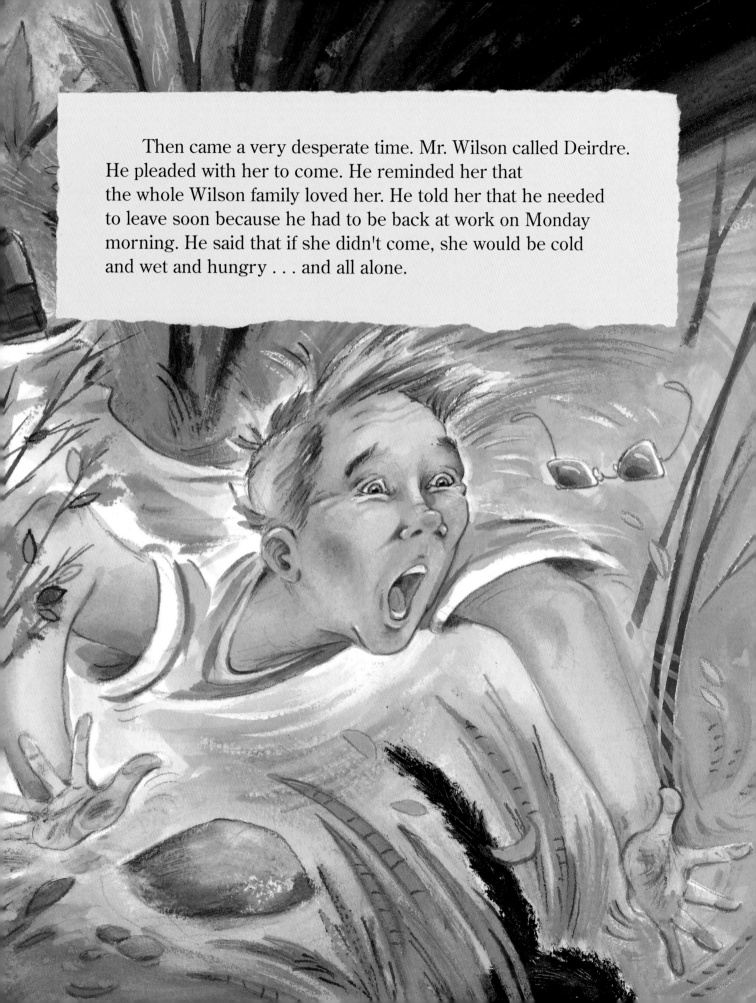

Then came a very desperate time. Mr. Wilson called Deirdre. He pleaded with her to come. He reminded her that the whole Wilson family loved her. He told her that he needed to leave soon because he had to be back at work on Monday morning. He said that if she didn't come, she would be cold and wet and hungry . . . and all alone.

Deirdre didn't pay any attention. She hated that cage. She hid under the thick bushes and wouldn't come out. Hours passed, and finally, Mr. Wilson had to leave. He was very, very sad, indeed.

Before Mr. Wilson left, he spoke to a man who lived in a nearby trailer. Then he talked to the Schuttenbeld family, who lived in a pretty white farmhouse across the highway. He told them the whole terrible story.

He said that his cat was black, but not like a Halloween cat. Halloween cats are black all over. Deirdre had three white spots on her tummy and under her chin. He explained about her split ear and her black leather nose. Before he left, he put Deirdre's cage in their barn.

Then, sore and full of misery, he started his long drive home.

Back home, everyone was upset when they heard what had happened. But Mr. Wilson was especially unhappy because he thought it was his fault that Deirdre had escaped. His family felt almost as sorry for him as for Deirdre or themselves. They tried not to cry too hard when he was around. It was a very gloomy household.

Each morning Mr. Wilson would wake up and think, "Oh dear, oh dear, oh Deirdre."

When Mrs. Wilson walked in the neighborhood, she was all alone. After a while she put Deirdre's food dishes in the garage, because they looked so empty on the kitchen floor.

When Marie was sick, Deirdre was not there to snuggle up against her knees.

When Kathryn returned from school there was no cat flopping down on the sidewalk for a tummy rub. And there was no cat waiting on the braided mat in the front hall.

In the meantime, a lot of people were looking for Deirdre. Every day the Schuttenbeld children went across the road to search for a black cat with a split ear, three white spots and a black leather nose. They took food. They called. There was no answer.

The man in the trailer looked up and down and around and about. But he didn't see Deirdre.

Word of Deirdre got to a church nearby. The minister loved cats. He put up a notice in the church vestibule. He told the whole Sunday school. He even made an announcement about Deirdre in church.

Mr. Wilson called the telephone operator and asked for the name of a store close to where Deirdre had escaped. He hoped they would put up a Lost Cat notice. The telephone operator loved cats, too. She did not charge Mr. Wilson for the call. Before she rang off, she said, "Try not to worry, and please let me know if you find her."

But it was hard not to worry when it was raining outside, or when the nights started to get cold. It was sad to look at the chair where Deirdre loved to snooze. Nobody felt like sitting in that chair.

As the days passed, the Wilsons kept wondering:
"Does she miss us as much as we miss her?"
"Where is she now?"

"If she tries to reach home, which home will she choose?"
"How far can an old cat walk before the snow comes?"

One cold October morning, Mrs. Schuttenbeld was drinking her coffee beside her window. She was thinking about Deirdre, when suddenly, she saw a black cat come out of the bushes. She rushed across the highway and called, "Here, Deirdre! Come here, Deirdre!"

Deirdre was tired of being alone. She wanted someone to stroke her head and rub her tummy. She hadn't purred in a very long time. So, she decided to come.

Mrs. Schuttenbeld looked at Deirdre. She saw the three white spots, the split ear, and the black, leather nose. She folded Deirdre in her arms and carried her back to the house. She put her where she would be safe and warm, and gave her something nice to eat. Then she phoned the Wilsons.

"We have your cat," she said.

Mr. Wilson was wild with excitement. He said he would arrange to have Deirdre picked up and put on an airplane.

"No," said Mrs. Schuttenbeld. "Tomorrow I will drive her to the airport myself."

She was a very kind lady.

Mr. Wilson picked Deirdre up the next day, but he did not open the cage. He put it in the car and Deirdre howled all the way home. When they arrived, Mr. Wilson opened the cage on the braided mat in the front hall.

The cat that came out was certainly Deirdre. But she was a whole lot of other things besides.

She had a sleek and velvet coat.

She had a lean and graceful body.

She walked like a queen with her head in the air.

Anyone at all — even a dog lover -- would have said that she was a very special cat.

For a whole month, Deirdre spent her nights on the bed, snuggled up to Mr. Wilson's knees. She had known he would bring her home. Still, it had been a long, long wait.

This is really and truly a true story.
I am Mrs. Wilson. Deirdre was our cat.
In fact, Deirdre is our cat.
Right now, she's waiting for Mr. Wilson
on the braided mat in the front hall.